Phan's Diary

Story by Louise Schofield

Illustrations by Meredith Thomas

PM Chapter Books
part of the Rigby PM Collection

U.S. edition © 2001 Rigby
a division of Reed Elsevier Inc.
1000 Hart Road
Barrington, IL 60010-2627
www.rigby.com

Text © 2001 Thomson Learning
Illustrations © 2001 Thomson Learning
Originally published in Australia by Thomson Learning

06 05 04 03 02
10 9 8 7 6 5 4 3 2

Phan's Diary
ISBN 0 7635 7789 8

Printed in China by Midas Printing (Asia) Ltd

Contents

Chapter 1   June 14 — 15   4

Chapter 2   June 16   8

Chapter 3   June 17 — 20   14

Chapter 4   June 21 — 23   18

Chapter 5   June 24 — 29   23

Chapter 6   June 30 — July 1   28

This fictional story is based on true stories told by Vietnamese refugees in the years following the Vietnam War. Journeys like the one described in this diary really took place.

Pronunciation of names:

Phan — Fung	*Bo (Dad) — Bo*
Hong — Hong	*Bà (Grandma) — Bu*
Huy — Hwi	*Ong (Grandpa) — Ong*
Ma (Mom) — Ma	

Chapter 1
June 14

I'm very sad tonight—so sad I don't know what to do. When Huy and Hong were asleep, my parents told me some very bad news.

We have to leave our home and travel to a new country. We're going on a long and dangerous journey in a boat—and we may never come back.

Bo says we're not safe here anymore. We have to go.

Tomorrow at midnight, Ma and Bo will wake me up. We'll go to the river and get in a boat with some other families. We can't take anything except for some food and a few clothes.

In the morning I'll say good-bye to Bà and Ong—my grandma and grandpa—but I can't say good-bye to my friends. If the soldiers find out what we are doing they might put us in jail. I can't tell anyone.

June 15

Today I am so sad that I feel sick. Bà wants me to eat well so I will be strong for the journey, but I'm not hungry. I don't even want any noodles.

When I said good-bye to Bà and Ong, I couldn't stop crying. Bà cried too, and when she hugged me she couldn't let me go. Then she gave me some candy to put in my pocket. It is my favorite kind of candy.

Ong says I have to be brave. He says that when I'm frightened at night I should look at the stars and remember that he and Bà can see those same stars, too.

I'm going to miss Ong and Bà very much.

Chapter 2

June 16

I'm on the boat now.

It's not easy writing here. The waves make the boat go up and down. Huy wanted to draw in my diary, but I told him that what I am writing is very important and I need to save the paper. He started crying, so I gave him one of Bà's candies. I gave Hong one too, a red one. It's her favorite color.

It seems as if we've been on this boat forever, but we left home just last night. I can't believe that we're never going back.

When we left at midnight to walk down to the river, our home looked like it always did. Huy's toys were in the sand out front.

Huy and Hong were asleep, so my parents carried them.

Last night, down on the riverbank, we waited in the dark, hoping no one would see us. There was no moon, and we weren't allowed to use any lights.

When a small boat came to pick us up, no one spoke at all. We just got in.

I was careful not to get my diary wet.

Our boat—Bo calls it the Freedom Boat—was waiting in the bay.

Soon after we got in, a patrol boat came by. I was very frightened. Customs officers asked my father for our papers. Luckily, Bo had false papers that said we were fishing people. The officers counted us and checked our papers. Then they left.

We waited in the dark. After a while we heard the sound of motors, although we couldn't see anything. Two small boats, like the one we had come in, arrived. When the people from those boats climbed onto the Freedom Boat, we sailed out of the bay. I watched until the lights on the land had disappeared.

I wonder if my friends will miss me.

Today we kept away from land. We didn't want to meet any more patrol boats. Huy and Hong were happy to be in the Freedom Boat at first, but after a while they wanted to go home and play. When they wouldn't stop crying, I promised to give them each a piece of candy tomorrow, and I played a game with them.

Chapter 3

June 17

It is scary on the boat at night. The waves are black and they seem so much bigger than in the daytime. Last night I found it difficult to sleep on the hard boards. There isn't much room.

When the sun is up, I'm hot and thirsty. We're allowed only one cup of water a day to drink.

There isn't much to eat.

June 18

Bo is worried. A boat that should have brought us more fuel has not come. Something has gone wrong. Soon we will have no motor, only the wind and the currents of the ocean.

Almost as bad, Bà's candies are almost gone. Whenever Huy and Hong have been frightened I've given them one, but now I'll save the last three for an emergency. I let Huy draw on the cover of my diary. He drew the Freedom Boat.

June 19

Today Bo caught some fish in a net.

"See," he said, "I really am a fisherman."

It's the first time I've seen him smile since we left home. Ma cooked the fish and we shared them with some of the other people on the boat. There wasn't much, but we all enjoyed it and afterward we sang songs together.

June 20

Last night there was a storm and everyone woke up. It was very frightening, and I felt sick. Then some people started screaming. Someone had fallen into the water.

We turned the boat around and everyone looked for the poor person, but we couldn't see anything. We called but no one answered back. All we could hear was the ocean and the wind and the rain.

We had to go on.

I am trying not to think about what happened to that person.

Chapter 4

June 21

Everything is going wrong. Yesterday we lost someone in the storm, and then today we were attacked by pirates.

When we saw their boat, we waved and called out to them. They came closer and then someone said that they were pirates. We tried to get away from them, but their boat was faster than ours.

When they came alongside us, some of them climbed in. They pushed people—even little children—and shouted and waved their arms. They made everyone give them money and jewelry. Ma gave them her only necklace. Bo gave them a ring and all our money.

When they left, Huy and Hong were screaming.

One man had a broken arm.

June 22

Last night I had a nightmare. In it, the pirates tried to take the last three candies in my pocket. When I woke, the candy was still there, but I was very frightened.

Then I remembered what Ong had said. I looked at the stars and remembered how much Ong and Bà love me.

I like to know that they can see the same stars, too.

We passed lots of islands today, and this morning we saw another boat. We thought we were going to be attacked by pirates again.

But this boat was a fishing boat, and the people on it were kind. They saw we were hungry and needed water and they gave us everything they could, including fish they had caught in their nets, and some fuel.

They invited us back to their village, but we had to go on.

June 23

Our journey is almost over. We are in the waters of a new country, and there is a refugee camp on an island nearby. Some of the people on the boat have relatives there.

Bo says we'll land there tomorrow.

Chapter 5
June 24

Today was terrible. This morning a patrol boat came up to us, and a man spoke to us through his loudspeaker. He told us we were not allowed to land on the island. We had to go away.

Bo shouted that some people had children in the refugee camp and that we were hungry and needed water. And that some people were sick.

The men on the boat didn't care. They still wouldn't let us land.

We didn't know where to go.

June 25

Last night was a bad night. Everyone was too tired and too sad to speak. Huy and Hong were exhausted, but at least they could sleep.

I lay awake all night listening to the waves.

The stars seemed closer, and I remembered what Ong told me—how I had to be brave. I'm trying. I really am.

I think of Ong and Bà and my friends a lot now. I miss them very much. I want to go home.

June 26

We're sailing on, looking for another place to go. No one will help us. Any fishing boats we see just sail away. Bo said they don't want to get into trouble. We saw two harbors today, but when we sailed toward them we were ordered away.

Why won't anyone help us? What will we do if no one lets us land?

June 27

Every day seems the same now. We don't talk much anymore. Even Huy and Hong are very quiet. We have very little water and our food is almost gone. No one wants us. The man with the broken arm is very sick.

June 28

We have no fuel now, and our boat is beginning to sink. We all have to take turns scooping the water out.

Huy, Hong, and I ate the last pieces of candy today. I sucked mine as slowly as I could to make it last forever. But nothing lasts that long.

I think this piece of candy might have been the last I'll ever eat. I feel very sad.

June 29

I helped scoop the water out again today. It gave me something to do. After a while my arm ached, and Bo took the cup from me. He hugged me and said he was proud of me.

He said, "Don't give up hope yet."

Chapter 6

June 30

Our Freedom Boat is really sinking. We are all scooping water faster than we were yesterday. I am trying not to lose hope, as Bo said, but I think this might be the last page of my diary. I don't think we can go on any longer.

But wait.

Someone is shouting that there is a boat!

Maybe someone will save us!

Now I can see it, too. It's a long way away. I hope they will see us.

Huy and Hong are frightened. They think it might be pirates. But Bo says that this is a big boat—too big for pirates.

July 1

Yesterday was the happiest day of my life. We were rescued!

I'm now sitting in the biggest ship I've ever seen. It's a ship from the American Navy. They saw us and helped us out of our sinking boat. It was a long climb up!

But they couldn't help our poor Freedom Boat. It's gone now. We got out of it just in time.

Huy and Hong are laughing again.

We've eaten good food—although there wasn't much rice—and we've had lots to drink.

Best of all, they gave the children some chocolate.

I don't know what will happen now, but I think we are safe. Bo says we are going to America. Maybe they'll let us stay there.

Tonight when I see the stars, I'll know that Ong and Bà are watching them, too. I'll tell them we're okay now. I did my best to be brave. And I want to tell them that we're on the biggest boat in the world!